SPELLBOUNNED

A Heart in the Trenches

First published by Spellbounned Publishing 2026

First edition

This book was professionally typeset on Reedsy.
Find out more at reedsy.com

Contents

Prologue 1
ONE 3
TWO 7
THREE 11
FOUR 17
FIVE 25
SIX 32
SEVEN 37
EIGHT 42
NINE 50
TEN 55
ELEVEN 59
TWELVE 64
THIRTEEN 68
FOURTEEN 72
FIFTEEN 77
A Sneak Peek at Book Two of the Midnight Calvary Trilogy… 82
Acknowledgments 84
About the Author 86
Also by Spellbounned 87

Prologue

You ever wake up from a dream drenched in cold sweat? A feverish chill runs from the tip of your toes to the tops of your earlobes. Painfully aware how eager you are to shake the feeling, yet you somehow find yourself paralyzed in that singular haunting moment.

A slow tick erupts inside your mind, like the countdown of a midnight pendulum clock.

3... 2... 1... A jolt!
Finally you break through. That eerie sensation dissipates followed by the ragged exhale of tired lungs. Your heart rate slows back into that deep steady rhythm. In and out, you breathe.

The phantom ticking fades into nothingness. Grounded by the steady rise and fall of your chest, you let your eyes close again, anchoring yourself to the solid, predictable safety of the waking world. The phantom terror of the dark is gone, vanquished by a simple breath. You are entirely exposed, yet entirely certain that the danger has passed.

But some forces don't need a nightmare to paralyze you. Some forces can steal the air right out of your lungs while you are wide awake.

You stare up at the ceiling, watching the familiar shadows of your room slowly reassemble themselves in the dark. The mundane world sneaks back in—the hum of the house, the cool press of the sheets, the comforting reality that the nightmare was just a trick of the mind. You convince yourself that you are safe. You wrap the silence around you like a shield, firmly back in the driver's seat of your own body.

But it's a fragile kind of peace. Because control is an illusion, a beautiful lie you tell yourself until the universe decides to remind you just how powerless you really are.

Losing control is never easy, but that's exactly how it feels when you lock eyes with Gideon Beaumont.

ONE

Uprooting my life was never a part of the plan. Moving an entire state away my senior year felt like a death sentence. The kind of nightmare you see on reality TV, where some unsuspecting teenager gets dragged kicking and screaming from their comfort zone for the sake of a "fresh start" they never asked for.

Leaving behind the calmness of the ocean was the hardest part. I was trading the steady, rhythmic peace of the cool waves for the wild, unpredictable wilderness. Every milestone I had anticipated—senior prom, walking the stage with friends I'd known since kindergarten, beach bonfires on warm summer nights was being torn away from me... replaced by a looming, dark canopy of trees.

My gaze shifts from the zooming white lines on the pavement, up to the terrified side profile of the woman I am supposed to call mom.

Her pale blue eyes are fixated on the road ahead, her knuckles white against the steering wheel. She has hardly said five words to me since she arrived in Buxton to drag me away from everything I have ever loved. The radio has been dead for hours, leaving only the low hum of the tires against the asphalt and the occasional heavy sigh to fill the space between us.

Three silent hours of anticipating the new hell I was about to be thrown into.

Charity was never cut out to be a mother. She left me with my father when I was fifteen months old, choosing her own freedom over a crying toddler. Years of therapy, meds, and gallons of tears wasted trying to understand why I wasn't enough. Eventually, I had come to accept that it was for the best. My dad and I had a routine. We had a life. I had convinced my self to leave the past behind me.

Turns out that seventeen years of freedom for her were over. My father is gone now… and my past is here to slap me right back into reality.

Watching my dad wither from the cancer eating away at him was the worst part of it all. They say the Morphine drip makes it painless, but as his body desperately hung on, I witnessed his soul slowly slipping away.

Day by excruciating day. He fought so hard to stay, while the woman driving this car couldn't wait to leave.

It is hard to describe the feelings I have now with every mile pulling me further from my home. A piece of myself is being left behind on the coast, slowly evaporating into the salt air while my body is forced onward.

Outside the passenger window, the bright coastal horizon has completely vanished, swallowed whole by an aggressive wall of dense pines and overgrown brush. The trees crowd the edge of the two-lane highway, casting long, eerie shadows across the hood of the car as the afternoon sun begins to dip.

ONE

The deeper we drive into the wilderness, the more suffocating it feels. The sky above is narrowing, trapped behind a ceiling of thick, tangled branches that block out the light.

Charity clears her throat, the sudden noise sharp enough to make me flinch. She doesn't look at me, but her fingers twitch on the wheel. "We're getting close," she murmurs, her voice raspy from hours of disuse. "Just a few more miles."

I don't answer. I just press my forehead against the cool glass of the window, watching the wild, dark woods blur past, waiting for the moment the tires finally turn off the main road.

The low hum of the engine feels loud in the heavy, unbroken silence of the car's cabin. With every mile we travel, the dense wilderness outside seems to edge even closer, as if the forest itself is trying to reclaim the narrow strip of asphalt beneath us. It feels less like a drive and more like a descent, burying me deep within the woods.

I watch Charity out of the corner of my eye. Her posture is stiff, her shoulders locked tight as she stares straight ahead through the windshield. Whatever thoughts are running through her mind, she isn't sharing them, and the distance between us feels much wider than the empty space between our seats.

Outside, the last remnants of the open sky disappear entirely. The ceiling of thick, tangled branches weaves tightly together overhead, plunging the highway into a premature, murky twilight. The air conditioning in the car suddenly feels too cold against my skin. I draw my jacket tighter around myself, trying to shake the uneasy sensation that the wilderness isn't just surrounding us, it is watching us.

The car slows down slightly as the highway begins to curve sharply, the headlights automatically flickering on to cut weak, yellow beams into the deepening gloom. Every twist in the road looks exactly like the last, an endless loop of ancient pines and overgrown brush that makes it feel as though we are driving in circles.

But then, Charity's foot moves to the brake. The rhythmic clicking of the turn signal suddenly punctuates the quiet, a sharp, predictable rhythm that signals the end of our highway journey. My heart gives a nervous, heavy thud against my ribs. I sit up a little straighter, my eyes straining against the darkness as the car slows to a crawl, poised at the very edge of a dirt road.

TWO

The sun was long gone by the time we pulled down the mile long dusty drive. The car slowed to a stop in front of an old mansion which had clearly long forgotten what proper landscaping was. The hedges grew wild. The flowerbeds overgrown with weeds, and a trail of poison oak stretched up to the second floor stoop.

There was a buzzing in the air, as the song of cicadas danced to my ears. The sky full of vivid stars, Mom turned to me with pain in her eyes...and just as I thought she would break the awkward silence she simply let out a deep sigh, squeezed my trembling fingers then exited the vehicle towards the house.

I was barely two steps over the threshold when I heard the thundering sound of pounding coming down the wood floors towards me. I turned just in time for two hairy paws to land on my shoulders. Ida, my grandmothers Irish wolf hound had to be the first to ease my sadness with her warm obnoxious kisses.

My eyes searched the dimly lit foyer. The dusty wallpaper was filled with old family portraits. The home dates back to the 1860's when my family first settled here in Virginia. Although the rooms are filled with elegant heirlooms, the house feels cold as if all the grandiosity degraded over the years of neglect. The bones are holding strong, but there is a hinting of secrets just below the surface.

I hear the call of my name resonating through the back side of the home. I follow the voice to the dark kitchen, then through to a regal room. There laying on the four poster bed surrounded by all sorts of medical equipment was my Nana. Slender and frail. She sat up to face my direction. She was still so hauntingly beautiful, her ruby red lips whispered for me to come closer.

I inched over to her side where she pulled me in close. Wrapping her arms tightly around my waist she spoke with a shaky voice...

"You know I would have been there." she said softly. Immediately followed by tears. My Nana was one of my biggest supporters growing up. She knew how hard it was for a single father to raise a little girl. She would send him money, and visit as much as she could. Two years ago things changed when Nana had a stroke. I never thought a woman so strong would crumble so rapidly. She spends every day in bed now, or in a wheelchair. The fiery passion she used to hold is slowly snuffing out. She took my hand in hers, and gave it a kiss on the backside. She called for Veronica her nurse. "Would you see that Clara gets settled in."

With that, I was sent to unpack the few belongings I had. Veronica led me up the winding stairs to the second floor. Every room we passed reminded me of a museum. Furniture had white sheets draped over them, photographs had a dusty hue, and there were candelabra chandeliers hanging from the high ceilings, casting skeletal shadows against the wallpaper.

Veronica stopped and opened an ornate wooden door. The

carvings on it were intricate and strangely mesmerizing, showing a dense woodland scene filled with various creatures and the unmistakable silhouette of a woman hidden among the trees. Behind it, the space opened up to an opulent room adorned with velvet bed linens that perfectly matched the deep maroon drapery pooling at the windows.

The stately room was unlike the others in the house. Everything here was pristine, not a speck of dust to be found. It felt prepared. Waiting.

My eyes focused on Veronica. "Thank you," I said, my voice sounding small in the vast space.

She looked me up and down, her expression unreadable for a moment, then gave a meek smile. "You are welcome, Clara. If you need anything at all, please just come find me or press this call button." She pointed to a small brass button built into a wooden box on the wall. With a quiet nod, she slipped away, her footsteps fading back down the hall to the stairs.

I walked over to the bed, pillowy and soft, and sat on the edge, gazing out the window toward the black night sky. I let out an exhausted sigh. For the first time since the funeral, I was finally alone.

The silence of the house pressed in on me, heavy and absolute. There was no hum of traffic here, no distant crash of the ocean waves I used to fall asleep to. Just the quiet creaking of an old estate settling into the night.

With heavy limbs, I dragged my small suitcase onto the mattress. Unpacking didn't take long—there wasn't much left to my name. I carefully set a few worn clothes into the dark wood wardrobe, the hinges groaning loudly in the quiet room. At the bottom of the bag lay a framed photograph of my father. My chest tightened as I traced the edge of the glass before placing it gently on the nightstand, his familiar smile a stark contrast to the cold, museum-like grandeur surrounding me.

I pulled the drapes blocking out the moonlight, plunging the room into a deep, velvety darkness. I stripped out of my travel-worn clothes, and slipped under the heavy maroon linens. The sheets were cool against my skin, and the mattress swallowed me whole.

I closed my eyes, intending to sort through the chaotic storm of thoughts in my head, but the sheer weight of grief and the endless miles of the road caught up to me. The darkness of the room seemed to bleed into my mind, pulling me under into a heavy, dreamless sleep before I could even finish another thought.

THREE

Warmth, followed by the fragrance of rich mahogany is what I remember waking up to after that first night. There was another smell I did not recognize, as it was overwhelmingly earthy. Disregarding the tickle in my nose, I forced myself out of bed. Crept over to the window, and to my surprise I realized my mothers bright red BMW was gone. Good, no unbearable silence to suffer through at breakfast. Mom works over at the Casino, her hours tend mirror her own unpredictability.

I threw on my sneakers, a baggy pair of jeans, white crop top, and my favorite baseball cap. Heading towards the door I grabbed my book bag containing my sketch pad, and pencils. Perhaps I could do some exploring today. I felt my excitement grow the closer I came to the end of the staircase. I was fumbling with my bag down the back hallway when I almost ran into Veronica! "I'm so sorry!" I exclaimed. She gave a cheeky grin, and continued down the hall with her basket of laundry.
Turning the corner to the kitchen, perched up on the counter was an enormous breakfast spread. I grabbed a bagel with

everything seasoning, slathered it with cream cheese, and shoved an orange in my bag. Rounding the center island I grabbed a water bottle before turning towards the back door. I was just reaching for the handle when Veronica came in the room. "Leaving so soon?" She mumbled while fiddling with the coffee pot. I turned, glancing over as the morning sun shone through the stained glass windows casting a rainbow on the floor before me. "Figured I could get to know my surroundings better." I chimed back.

"Of course! Please be back before sunset, your Nana wants to have a family dinner to welcome you home." She rose her hand giving a pleasant wave. Which was returned by my wary smile as I shuffled out the door.

The morning breeze wrapped its brisk arms around me. Sunlight warmed my skin, but glancing around the fog created an eerie sensation. A mystery of where the day could take me lingering in the air. Deep breaths. I head off towards a path in the treeline. The sounds of squirrels jumping, and chattering through the trees ring up to my ears. Following close behind are the sounds of what must be a creek. Pushing further through the brush, I find myself at the edge of a stream. The water opens up to a clearing. I follow the bank down to some large rocks. I paused for a moment, looking around to take in all of the colors of the foliage. Then continued on my pursuit of adventure. I eventually came to the edge of a long dirt trench on the edge of the woods. Climbing over it revealed a cemetery. The cemetery is older than the trees surrounding it, a forgotten pocket of history swallowed by the Virginia wilderness. Weathered headstones jut out from the overgrown grass like broken teeth, their inscriptions long erased by time and moss. A heavy, reverent quiet hangs here, dampening the chatter of the squirrels I left behind by the creek.

I pull my sketchbook and charcoal pencil from my bag, the familiar weight settling the restless energy in my chest. Finding a flat, moss-covered stone near the center of the clearing, I sit down and let my eyes wander until they land on a particularly crooked marker shadowed by a massive, ancient oak tree.

My pencil meets the paper. *Scratch. Scratch. Scratch.*

The rhythmic sound is comforting. I lose myself in the lines, capturing the jagged edges of the stone and the way the morning fog seems to pool around its base like water. I'm so focused on shading the deep grooves of the oak's bark that it takes me a moment to realize the birds have completely stopped singing.

The silence isn't peaceful anymore. It's heavy. Expectant.

A shadow falls across my page.

I freeze, my pencil hovering millimeters above the paper. The air grows suddenly thick, carrying a scent that makes the hairs on my arms stand up—a sharp mix of damp earth, pine resin, and something deeply, undeniably wild.

"You shouldn't be sketching the dead. They don't like to be reminded of what they lost."

The voice deep, a low rumble that vibrates right through the stone beneath me.

My breath hitches as I look up. Standing at the edge of the oak tree's shadow isn't a ghost. He is massive, towering well over six feet, his broad silhouette nearly blocking out the morning sun filtering through the canopy. Yet, despite his size, he hadn't made a single sound crossing the brush. His features are a striking, but his blue eyes lock onto mine with an intensity that pins me to the spot.

He steps forward, the sunlight catching the edge of his form. I swallow hard, gripping my sketchbook a little tighter. "I'm pretty sure the dead don't mind a little charcoal."

A faint, unreadable expression crosses his face, gone as quickly as it appeared. He steps closer, his movements fluid and entirely silent. "You're new here. People from town usually avoid this ridge. They say the woods play tricks on your mind."

"I'm not easily tricked," I say, trying to sound braver than I feel. The sheer presence of him is overwhelming, commanding the entire clearing. "And it's just a cemetery. A bit overgrown, but peaceful."

"Peaceful," he echoes, a strange, hollow edge to his voice. He looks around at the weathered headstones, his gaze lingering on them with a familiarity that makes my chest tighten. "I suppose it looks that way from the outside."

Before I can ask him what he means, he looks back down at me, his eyes first scanning my face, then tracking down to the drawing in my lap. "You have a gift. But you should be careful how far into the treeline your 'pursuit of adventure' takes you."

A chill runs down my spine. Did he hear me talking to myself earlier?

I look down at my sketchbook for a fraction of a second, my mind racing, and when I look back up to demand an answer, the words catch in my throat.

He's already gone.

I scramble to my feet, spinning around to look at the edge of the woods. The brush is completely still. No rustling leaves, no heavy footsteps echoing through the trees. It's as if he simply dissolved back into the afternoon fog.

A sudden, sharp vibration in my pocket breaks the silence, making me jump. I pull out my phone. A text from my mom flashes on the screen, a stark reminder of the world outside this clearing: *Nana's having the table prepared. Don't be late for dinner!*

The spell of the cemetery breaks instantly. Panic replaces my confusion as I realize how late it's gotten.

Shoving my sketchbook and pencils into my bag, I scramble back over the long dirt trench and race toward the path by the stream. The brisk morning air has turned into a warm afternoon breeze, but the memory of those blue eyes keeps me cold all the way back. By the time I break through the treeline and sprint up the porch steps of the house, I'm breathless, my heart pounding like thunder against my ribs.

I throw open the front door, the rich, savory scent of roasted chicken and garlic immediately wrapping around me. From the kitchen, the clinking of silverware and the bright sound of Nana's laughter drift down the hall.

I take one deep, steadying breath, trying to shake the dust of the woods from my clothes. My hands are still slightly trembling from the adrenaline of my run, and my sneakers are caked in dark, damp earth. Hanging my heavy bag on the coat rack near the door, I quickly brush my palms down the front of my jeans, desperately trying to sweep away any stray twigs or dried leaves before anyone notices where I've been.

The warmth of the house is almost overwhelming compared to the chilling atmosphere of the cemetery clearing. The hallway floorboards groan softly under my weight as I take a few tentative steps toward the source of the noise. The light spilling out from the dining room is amber and inviting, casting long shadows of the heavy, antique furniture against the walls.

I can hear the murmur of voices rising in pitch, the sharp clink of a serving spoon hitting porcelain, and the rustle of fabric. My stomach gives a nervous twist. I don't want to answer questions about why I'm late, and I certainly don't want to explain what I found out there by the stream.

Smoothing down my hair and forcing my features into what I hope looks like a calm expression, I step forward into the bright light of the doorway to meet my family.

FOUR

Family dinners always gave me an uneasy feeling. Since my dad was gone I guess the thought of pretending always sent my head into a tail spin.

I mean, how can you fake a smile when you feel as though you've stepped into an alternate reality. My brain disassociates from my body, but I smile anyway. Poising myself on the edge of the velvet dinner chair I find myself fiddling with the elegant silverware. My fingers trace the edges sliding down the cool metal.

My trance is broken by a sharp elbow to my side as my mother tries to bring my attention back to the topic of conversation tonight… me.

Clara, sweetie, did you hear your Nana?" My mother's voice cuts through my fog, her sharp elbow still lingering near my ribs. She smiles tightly, the kind of look that silently pleads with me to *just be normal* for one night.

Across the table, Nana sets down her wine glass, her eyes warm but searching. "I was just saying, Clara, it must be quite an adjustment moving out here to Dinwiddie right before your senior year. Have you had a chance to look around yet? Find any inspiration for those beautiful sketches of yours?"

My heart does a strange, violent thud against my ribs as the hidden cemetery flashes behind my eyelids. Those piercing blue eyes. The impossible silence of a six-foot-plus stranger vanishing into thin air.

"I… yeah," I stammer, clearing my throat and adjusting my napkin. "I took a walk down by the creek earlier. It's definitely different than back home. Very quiet."

"Quiet is good for the soul," Nana says softly, though a shadow of something older and more cautious passes over her face. "But do stick to the main paths, darling. These old Virginia woods… well, the terrain can be tricky if you don't know your way around. Especially up near the old ridge lines."

The ridge. Exactly where he said people from town avoid.

"Is there something up there?" I ask, trying to keep my voice casual as I cut into my chicken.

"Just old history," my mother interjects quickly, a little too loudly, as if trying to steer the ship away from a rocky shoreline. "Civil War skirmishes, old overgrown properties. Nothing for a teenager to worry about. Let's focus on Monday. Are you nervous about starting at the high school?"

The topic shifts, the velvet chairs feel a little more suffocating, and I spend the rest of the night nodding along, pretending to care about school supply lists while my mind remains firmly anchored in the damp, quiet woods.

Three days pass in a blur of cardboard boxes and restless nights. Every time I close my eyes, I see a flash of brilliant, piercing blue.

By the time Monday morning rumbles around, the eerie

mystery of the cemetery is eclipsed by a brand-new flavor of dread: the first day of senior year at Dinwiddie High.

The school looks exactly how you'd expect a rural Virginia high school to look, low-slung brick buildings, a parking lot dominated by mud splattered pickup trucks, and a thick humidity that makes my new school clothes stick to my skin. Navigating the crowded hallways feels like walking through an alternate universe. Everyone here has known each other since kindergarten. They share inside jokes, navigate the halls in tight knit packs, and cast curious, lingering glances at the new girl clutching a crinkled schedule like a lifeline.

By third period, my brain is completely fried from answering the same three questions: *Where did you move from? Why did you come here? Are you related to the Beaumonts down the road?*

I slide into a desk in the back row of my English Literature class, dropping my backpack onto the floor with a heavy sigh. The room smells like old paper and cheap floor wax. I pull out my sketchbook, hiding it beneath a textbook, and mindlessly begin to shade the outline of an ancient oak tree, trying to ground myself.

The warning bell rings, a harsh metallic buzz that makes everyone scramble for their seats.

"Alright, settle down," the teacher calls out, shuffling a stack of syllabus papers. "Before we get started on the reading list, we have a couple of schedule adjustments this morning."

The classroom door clicks open.

I don't look up immediately, too busy perfecting the jagged edge of a headstone on my page. But then, a sudden, heavy stillness settles over the entire room. The chatter dies instantly.

A sharp, electric chill zaps up my spine—the exact same sensation I felt in the foggy clearing three days ago.

I slowly raise my head.

Standing in the doorway, a canvas backpack slung carelessly over one shoulder, is the tall, rugged boy from the woods. Cleaned up in a dark t-shirt and jeans, he looks entirely normal yet he still possesses that same commanding, presence that makes the classroom feel suddenly very small.

His sharp gaze sweeps across the rows of students, completely indifferent to the hushed whispers breaking out around him. Then, his eyes lock onto mine.

Those piercing blue eyes hit me like a physical blow. A faint, knowing smirk tugs at the corner of his mouth, and my breath catches completely in my throat.

"Class," the teacher says, oblivious to the panic dynamic exploding in the back row. "This is Gideon. Gideon Beaumont. Find an open seat, please."

Gideon doesn't break eye contact with me as he steps into the aisle, his movements entirely fluid and silent, heading straight for the empty desk right next to mine.

The wooden legs of Gideon's chair scrape silently against the floor as he slides in next to me. He doesn't look at me again. He just stares straight ahead at the chalkboard, his large hands folded on the desk, the dark fabric of his t-shirt stretched tight across his broad shoulders.

I, on the other hand, am falling apart. My hand shakes so badly I can barely hold my charcoal pencil. I try to stare at my textbook, but my peripheral vision is entirely consumed by him. He's right here. The mysterious stranger from the hidden cemetery, sitting in third period English.

The teacher begins droning on about the syllabus, but I can't process a single word. Slowly, carefully, I lean a fraction of an inch in his direction.

FOUR

"How did you do that?" I whisper, my voice barely a breath.

Gideon doesn't move a muscle. For a second, I think he's going to ignore me entirely. Then, without turning his head, his deep voice cuts through the ambient noise of the classroom, pitched so low only I can hear it. "Do what?"

"In the woods," I hiss, looking down at my desk so the teacher doesn't catch me talking. "Three days ago. You vanished. You didn't make a sound."

A subtle shift ripples through him, a tightening of his jaw. He finally turns his head, those piercing blue eyes locking onto me, cold and unyielding. "I told you, the woods play tricks on your mind. You shouldn't have been up on the ridge, Clara."

My heart stops. *Clara.*

"I never told you my name," I whisper, the blood rushing in my ears.

A faint, dangerous smirk touches his lips, but before he can answer, the teacher's voice booms out. "Mr. Beaumont? Miss Clara? Is there something you'd like to share with the rest of the class?"

Gideon pulls his gaze away from me smoothly. "No, sir. Just getting caught up on the reading list."

The rest of the period passes in an agonizing, silent standoff. When the bell finally rings, Gideon is out of his seat and gone before I can even zip my backpack. He moves like wind through the crowded hallway, disappearing into the sea of teenagers before I can catch up.

By fifth period, my nerves are completely shot. I practically collapse into the art studio, a bright, messy room that smells of a comforting mixture of acrylic paint, turpentine, and clay. It's the first place all day that feels like a sanctuary.

I find a tall stool at an empty wooden worktable in the back, pulling my sketchbook out to look at the oak tree I'd been drawing.

"Oh my gosh, did you draw that? That is *insanely* good!"

A whirlwind of bright energy drops into the stool right next to mine. The girl has a bouncy blonde ponytail, perfectly manicured nails, and a vibrant smile that instantly commands the room. She's wearing a varsity cheerleader jacket, but she doesn't have the icy vibe you'd expect. She oozes pure warmth.

"I'm Sabrina, by the way," she says, extending a hand that jingles with silver bracelets. "But everyone calls me Bree. You're the new girl, right? Clara?"

"Yeah, that's me," I say, a bit breathless from her speed, but genuinely smiling for the first time all day. "Nice to meet you, Bree."

"Seriously, your shading is beautiful," another voice chimes in from across the table.

I look up to see a girl sitting opposite us. She has a completely different vibe than Bree—effortlessly cool, with long, ink-black hair braided down her back and sharp, intelligent dark eyes. Her hands are stained faintly with some kind of green herbal residue, and she wears an intricate beaded silver ring on her thumb.

"I'm Rowan," she says with a calm, grounding smile. "Don't let Bree overwhelm you. She runs on pure espresso and school spirit."

"Hey! I do not," Bree laughs, shoving Rowan's shoulder playfully. "I run on iced matcha. Get it right."

Rowan rolls her eyes affectionately, turning back to me. "I saw you walking down by the creek trail the other day, near the old tree line. You looked a little lost."

A prickle of familiarity touches the back of my neck. "Yeah, I was just exploring. Trying to get a feel for the town."

Rowan's eyes hold mine for a beat longer than necessary. There is an ancient, knowing depth to her gaze, a sharp contrast to Bree's bubbly innocence. "Just be careful around here, Clara. Dinwiddie has deep roots, and some of the history around these parts doesn't like to be disturbed. Especially the further in the woods you go."

I glance down at my sketch of the cemetery, then back up at Rowan's serious expression and Bree's cheerful grin. For the first time since I moved to Virginia, I feel a sudden spark of hope. I might be completely out of my depth with Gideon Beaumont, but looking at the two girls sitting with me, I have a feeling I'm not going to have to face the mysteries of this town alone.

The conversation drifts into lighter territory after that, standard high school gossip and complaints about upcoming assignments, but Rowan's words remain anchored in the back of my mind. We stay until the art teacher begins wiping down the adjacent tables and stacking the chairs, a silent cue that our afternoon reprieve has come to an end.

We exchange numbers on the sidewalk outside, the cool evening air settling over Dinwiddie as the streetlights flicker to life. Bree gives me a quick, enthusiastic hug, promising to text me the details for lunch tomorrow, while Rowan offers a softer, parting smile that feels like a quiet reassurance.

Watching them walk away together, I finally turn back toward home.

The rest of Monday night passes in a dull, quiet blur. Dinner with my family is a mechanical affair—chewing, swallowing, answering questions about my day with vague, practiced pleasantries while my thoughts remain locked away in the dense woods by the creek. Up in my bedroom, I slip the sketchbook into my desk drawer, sliding it beneath a stack of loose notebook paper as if hiding it could somehow dull the restless curiosity burning in my chest.

When I finally crawl into bed, the silence of the old estate feels heavier than usual. Rowan's warning echoes in the quiet spaces of the room: *some of the history around these parts doesn't like to be disturbed.* I stare up at the dark ceiling, watching the shadows of the tree branches sway against the window glass like reaching fingers, wondering what exactly is waiting out there in the dark. It takes hours for my racing mind to finally quiet down, eventually slipping into a heavy, dreamless sleep.

FIVE

The Tuesday morning sun does nothing to burn off the damp chill clinging to the brick walls of Dinwiddie High. I sit in English class, shivering slightly in my jacket and tracing a mindless pattern onto the laminate wood of my desk. My eyes keep drifting, inevitably fixing on the empty desk next to mine. Gideon is late. Or maybe he's skipping entirely. After our whispering match yesterday, I wouldn't blame him if he decided to avoid this room—and me—altogether.

Around me, the classroom is a loud, chaotic hum of morning chatter. Students are trading complaints about weekend homework, laughing over inside jokes, and slamming locker keys onto their desks. I feel like an outside observer watching a movie on mute, my mind still locked onto the heavy secrets buried in the woods.

Suddenly, the bell rings, its harsh metallic buzz cutting through the chatter and vibrating straight through my teeth.

"Alright, settle down," Mr. Harrison calls out, his voice instantly dropping a blanket of reluctant quiet over the room.

He raps a piece of chalk sharply against the blackboard, leaving a dusty white streak in its wake. "Quiet down and get to your seats. Today we are starting our multi-week historical research project. You'll be working in pairs to dig into Dinwiddie's local history, specifically, the domestic impact of the Civil War campaigns in 1865."

A collective groan ripples through the classroom, accompanied by the dramatic slumping of several heads onto desks. Across the room, Bree catches my eye and mouths the word *tragic* with a theatrical roll of her eyes.

"Yes, yes, save your tears for the grading rubric," Mr. Harrison says dryly, ignoring the protests as he pulls a heavily annotated, sheet of paper from his podium. He adjusts his glasses, squinting down at the handwritten grid. "I've already assigned your partners, so there will be no negotiating, no trading, and absolutely no working alone. Bree, you're with Caleb Finch. Rowan, you're with Silas Vance..."

I perk up at the names, my attention snapping tightly back to the front of the room. Caleb and Silas—those are the two guys I keep seeing leaning against a mud-splattered pickup truck in the parking lot every single morning, looking like they stepped straight out of a rugged backcountry catalog. I glance over at Rowan, but her expression is completely unreadable, her gaze locked forward.

Mr. Harrison's finger slides down the ledger, his voice droning on as he pairs up the rest of the class. My chest tightens with a sudden, nervous dread. There are only a few names left.

"...And Clara, you'll be paired with Gideon Beaumont."

A few subtle whispers break out near the back row, but before I can even process the weight of the assignment or figure out how I'm supposed to partner with a ghost, a sudden sound cuts through the room.

Right on cue, the classroom door clicks open. Gideon steps inside, his tall, rugged frame instantly casting a long shadow across the threshold. Cleaned up in a dark crewneck, he still carries that impossible, silent gravity. He doesn't look at the teacher. He just walks straight to his desk and slides into the seat next to mine.

"Mr. Beaumont, glad you could join us," Mr. Harrison sighs. "You and Clara are focusing on the 1865 ridge line skirmishes."

As the teacher turns back to the board, I lean slightly toward Gideon. "Looks like we're partners."

Gideon doesn't turn his head. He pulls a blank notebook from his bag, his large hands moving with a precise, deliberate calm. "I'll do the research on the military archives. You can write the summary. We don't need to meet up."

His voice is just as deep as I remember, a low rumble.

"Wow, don't overwhelm me with your team spirit," I whisper back, a spark of frustration overriding my nerves. "Why are you so determined to not get to know me? Or pretend that you didn't do a disappearing act in the woods?"

Gideon pauses, his pen hovering over the paper. Slowly, he turns his head. Up close, his piercing blue eyes are so intense it feels like a physical pressure in the room. "I told you to stay away from the ridge, Clara. I meant it. For your own safety, do your half of the project, and don't push your luck."

Before I can snap back, his gaze drops to my desk. My sketchbook is open to a fresh drawing of the ancient oak tree from the cemetery. But as I was daydreaming earlier, my hand had mindlessly traced a strange geometric symbol into the bark—a jagged, interlocking pattern I didn't even realize I was drawing.

Gideon's jaw clenches so hard a muscle twitches in his cheek. The icy blue of his eyes darkens.

"Where did you see that?" he demands, his voice dropping to a harsh, dangerous whisper.

"I… I don't know," I stammer, caught off guard by his sudden intensity. "I just drew it."

He stares at the symbol for a fraction of a second longer, a look of profound, ancient worry crossing his features, before he abruptly shuts his notebook. He doesn't say another word for the rest of the period. The bell rings.. perfect because I need food fuel to clear this frustration before sacred art class.

"He is literally impossible," I vent, slamming my tray down on the cafeteria table.

Bree giggles, tossing her bouncy blonde ponytail over her shoulder. "Oh, come on, Gideon is just… brooding. It's a Beaumont family trait. But honestly, you should see him when he's around Silas and Caleb. They're like a package deal. It's almost creepy how close they are like they have their own secret language or something."

Across the table, Rowan is quietly sorting through a small leather pouch of dried leaves, dropping a few into her water bottle. Her dark eyes look up, locking onto mine. "They've lived on that ridge a long time, Bree. Old families share old secrets."

"Well, Caleb everyone calls him Pip, by the way—is actually being sweet about the project," Bree says, leaning in logistically. "He wants to show me some old family maps this weekend."

"Just be careful up there," Rowan says softly, her voice taking on a grounding, serious weight. "Both of you. The energy on the ridge line has been shifting lately. It feels… heavy. Like a storm is coming."

FIVE

Bree laughs it off, shifting the conversation to Friday's football game, but Rowan catches my eye. She tilts her head toward the cafeteria doors. "Clara. Let's go for a walk after school today, I'd love to show you something." Holding her stare I agreed. The rest of the day is a slow burn. I stare at the clock as the minutes drag on.

After school, Rowan takes me to her family's apothecary shop on the edge of town. The moment we walk in, the scent of dried lavender, crushed pine needles, and rich earth wraps around me, instantly soothing the raw edge of my nerves.

Rowan walks behind the counter and disappears into a back room, returning a moment later with a heavy, fragile book bound in weathered leather.

"My family has been in this valley for generations," Rowan says, laying the journal gently on the wooden table between us. "My great-great-grandmother was a healer during the Civil War. She kept records of the things the history books left out."

She opens the fragile pages, flipping past recipes for poultices and tinctures until she stops on a page dated *April 1865*.

My breath hitches.

There, drawn in faded iron-gall ink, is the exact same geometric symbol I had sketched in English class.

"What is it?" I whisper, my fingers hovering just above the page.

"It's a ward," Rowan says, her voice low and reverent. "According to my grandmother's journals, a dark shadow came to Dinwiddie during the final days of the war. A man, an occultist, a soldier of fortune—who used a corrupted, ancient blood magic to turn the dying on the battlefield into something monstrous. He wanted an army of unstoppable beasts."

Staring at the images, a chill zaps straight up my spine. "Bigfoot... Sasquatch... they aren't just animals. They're cursed?"

Rowan nods solemnly. "Our tribes called them Stone Coats or Bukwas. The journal says three Union soldiers were changed right before the war ended. They managed to break free from his control, using this very ward to drive the shadow away. But the magic required a blood bond to keep the curse contained. They became the Midnight Calvary."

My mind races, pieces of a terrifying puzzle slamming together in my head. *Three soldiers.* They've been protecting this town since 1865.

"But if you say the shadow 'was' sealed..." I start, my voice trembling.

"The seal is weakening," Rowan interrupts, looking out the front window of the shop. "I've seen shadows roaming the edge of the woods."

A sudden, overwhelming sensation of being watched makes me turn my head toward the glass.

Standing across the street, completely enveloped in the fading twilight, is Gideon. He stands entirely still, his broad silhouette cutting a formidable shape against the darkening sky. Through the glass, his piercing blue eyes lock onto mine. There is no anger in them now—only a silent, desperate warning.

A shadow passes over the street, a cold wind rattling the apothecary door, and in the blink of an eye, Gideon dissolves back into the darkness, leaving me shivering in the light of the shop.

My breath hitches, and I press a hand flat against the glass, staring out at the empty space where he had just been standing. The street is completely vacant now, save for a few dead leaves swirling across the asphalt. It's as if he evaporated into the very air.

FIVE

"Clara?" Rowan's voice breaks through my paralysis, her hand gently touching my shoulder. She looks out the window, her brow furrowed with deep concern. "Did you see something?"

"Gideon," I breathe, finally finding my voice, though it sounds incredibly weak. "He was right there. He was looking right at me."

Rowan's grip tightens on my shoulder, her expression hardening. "It is just your mind playing tricks, Clara. You know that, right?"

I can only nod, the chilling reality of her words settling deep into my bones. The rest of our conversation passes in a tense, hushed whisper as we lock up the shop, but my mind remains firmly fixed on those piercing blue eyes.

When I finally return home, the old house feels colder than usual. I spend the entire night tossing and turning beneath my heavy blankets, the ancient lore of 1865 and the image of Gideon's silhouette playing on a maddening loop behind my eyelids. Sleep is a lost cause. Every creak of the floorboards or rustle of the wind outside my window sounds like a shadow creeping closer to the estate.

By the time the alarm on my phone finally rings, my eyes are burning and my mind is practically fracturing under the weight of a hundred unanswered questions. I don't just want answers anymore—I *need* them. If three soldiers were changed back in 1865, there has to be a paper trail. A record, a town archive, an old newspaper—something tangible left behind in the history books to prove I haven't completely lost my mind.

I pull myself out of bed with a newfound, desperate resolve. The second I get to school, I'm bypassing the morning social circles. I need old records, and I know exactly where to find them.

SIX

The fluorescent lights of the county library hum with a low, irritating buzz that matches the dull ache in my temples. Everyone decided to meet up here to begin our local history research, and the room is a chaotic mess of squeaking chairs, whispered gossip, and the musty scent of old paper.

I sit at a secluded wooden table in the very back corner, hidden behind a towering shelf of encyclopedias. Spread out in front of me is a heavy binder of local historical archives and a stack of printed microfiche records about Dinwiddie's 1865 campaigns.

A shadow falls across my desk.

I don't even have to look up to know who it is. The air around the table instantly shifts, turning heavy and thick with that familiar, wild scent of damp earth and herbs. Gideon slides his massive frame into the plastic chair next to mine. The chair groans under his weight, looking entirely too small for him. He doesn't look at me, nor does he say a word. He simply pulls a massive, yellowed book on Virginia topography from his canvas bag, opens it to a marked page, and buries himself in the text.

Ten minutes pass. Then twenty. The silence stretching between us is agonizing, a physical wall I can't seem to break through. He moves with a precise, deliberate calm, flipping pages without making a single sound. It's infuriating.

Frustrated, I rip a blank sheet of paper from my spiral notebook. I press my pen hard into the page and write: *Why are you looking at me like I'm a ghost?*

I slide the paper across the wooden table, tapping my finger against it.

Gideon's hand pauses above his book. Slowly, his sharp gaze tracks over to the note. He stares at my handwriting for a long beat, his jaw tightening. Then, he reaches into his pocket, pulls out a heavy, antique-looking fountain pen, and writes directly beneath my words.

He slides the paper back. His handwriting is stunning—an elegant, sweeping, old-fashioned cursive that looks like it belongs in a museum, not on a piece of lined notebook paper.

I shouldn't be looking at all.

My eyes shoot up abruptly, and lock into his stare. Heat flushes over my cheeks, followed by the woozy feeling of my stomach to the floor. A feeling I would never expect to from Gideon. A wave of curiosity washes over me. I grip my pen tighter as I search my brain for a reply, but before my nib can touch the paper, a bright voice cuts through our corner of the library.

"Oh, thank goodness, I found you guys! The fiction section is a literal maze."

Bree slides into the seat across from us, as she drops a massive stack of historical volumes onto the table. *THUMP.*

The sound is loud, echoing sharply against the library walls.

What happens next takes a fraction of a second, but it sends a cold shiver straight down my spine. At the exact moment the books hit the wood… Silas, and Pip who had been quietly following Bree over to the table along with Gideon all flinch in perfect, terrifyingly fast unison. Their shoulders square, their spines go rigid as iron, and their hands instantly drop to their sides, their bodies tensing almost like they've just responded to a gunshot on a battlefield.

It does not feel like a normal startled reaction. It was instinct.

"Whoa, sorry," Bree whispers, casting an amused look at the boys as Silas and Pip quickly relax, sliding into the remaining chairs. "Didn't mean to give you guys a heart attack."

"You're fine, Bree-Bree," Pip says, offering a lazy, charming smile as he pulls a map of the 1865 Battle of Dinwiddie Court House toward himself. He traces a thumb over a faded blue line representing the old Union trenches. "Man, the mud on that ridge was an absolute nightmare that April. Couldn't get the horses through it to save our lives…"

Silas sharply clears his throat, his heavy boot making a distinct *crack* as it connects with Pip's shin under the table.

Pip winces, his face going pale as he abruptly cuts himself off, swallowing hard.

I frown, staring across the table at them. *That April?* The way Pip said it didn't sound like he was reading a quote from a diary. It sounded like a memory. I look over at Gideon, expecting him to make a joke, but his face is cast in stone. He is glaring at Pip with a dark, warning intensity that makes the air feel suddenly freezing.

"You're reading the wrong map, Pip," Gideon says, his voice dropping to a low, commanding baritone that carries a weight no ordinary teenager could mimic. "That was a century ago.

Focus on the text."

"Right. Yeah. The text," Pip mutters, staring intently down at his book, completely silenced.

I glance at Rowan, who is sitting quietly at the end of the table. She isn't looking at the maps. She is looking at me, her dark, intelligent eyes tracking the confusion on my face. She gives me a tiny, almost imperceptible shake of her head, a silent warning to let it go.

I look down at my notebook, my mind spinning as I trace the elegant, old-fashioned cursive Gideon left on my page. I don't know what kind of secret these boys are keeping, but as I sneak a glance at Gideon's icy blue eyes. I feel as though suddenly the history isn't just in these books.

It could be sitting right next to me...

The heavy silence stretches between us, thick and uncomfortable. Pip keeps his eyes glued to the map, his fingers nervously tracing the faded ink border as if trying to physically erase his slip of the tongue. Beside him, Gideon doesn't move. He remains perfectly still, a statue of quiet menace, until the sharp, mechanical tick of the library's wall clock seems to snap him back to the present.

He blinks, the chilling intensity fading from his eyes just enough to let the ambient warmth of the room creep back in. "We should wrap this up," Gideon says, his voice smooth now, though the authoritative edge hasn't entirely vanished. "The library closes in twenty minutes, and the weather is turning."

Rowan is the first to move, her practical nature taking over. She begins stacking her reference books with deliberate, noisy efficiency, breaking the last remnants of the spell that had held us paralyzed. "He's right," she says smoothly, her tone perfectly conversational, though she still avoids looking directly at me.

"The forecast said the front would hit by this evening. I'd rather not get caught in a downpour on the walk home."

"Yeah. Good idea," Pip mumbles. He closes his textbook with a dull thud, looking thoroughly chastised and eager to escape.

I force my hands to stop trembling as I pack away my notebook, the loops of Gideon's handwriting still burned into my mind. I try to catch Rowan's eye again, wanting to press her for answers, but she is entirely focused on zipping her backpack. When I look up, Gideon is already standing. He slings his jacket over one shoulder, giving me a polite, entirely unreadable nod that feels a million miles away from the intense gaze of just a few moments ago.

"See you, Clara," he says softly.

"See you." I reply, the words tasting like ash in my mouth.

We part ways at the heavy oak doors of the library. Outside, the air has turned bitter and damp, the scent of ozone and oncoming rain hanging heavy over the concrete. The sky is a bruised, twilight purple, heavy clouds churning violently overhead as the wind begins to whip through the trees.

By the time I make it back to the safety of my own house, the first fat drops of rain are already slamming against the pavement. I lock the door behind me, though home offers little comfort against the storm brewing both outside and inside my own mind. As the wind begins to rattle the windowpanes, I know I won't be getting any sleep tonight.

SEVEN

A heavy storm slams into Dinwiddie over the weekend, turning the sky an ominous slate gray and lashing the trees with sheets of torrential rain. The power in Nana's house flickers once before dying completely, leaving the hallway cast in shadows.

I retreat to the covered back porch, wrapping a cozy blanket tight around my shoulders. The air is thick with the scent of petrichor, and ozone. With my sketchbook propped on my knees, I watch the rain turn the yard into a blur of green and gray. But my mind is miles away, stuck in the library. That elegant cursive looping across my brain: *I shouldn't be looking.*

I let my charcoal pencil wander across the page, mindlessly trying to capture the raw power of the storm.

Then, my heart stops.

Through the thick curtain of rain, near the edge of the property where the lawn surrenders to the dense wilderness of the woods, a dark silhouette is standing. He isn't wearing a jacket or holding an umbrella. He's just standing there, completely unbothered by the downpour, his broad frame cutting a formidable shape against the thrashing trees.

Gideon.

Driven by a sudden rush of adrenaline, I drop my sketchbook onto the porch chair, grab my umbrella from the stand by the door, and sprint out into the storm.

"Gideon!" I yell over the roaring thunder, the grass squelching beneath my slippers.

By the time I reach him, the wind is turning my umbrella inside out, but he doesn't even blink. He stands entirely still, his eyes fixed on the dark, distant ridge line. Rain drips from his jaw, plastering his dark hair to his forehead, but when he slowly turns his head to look at me, his piercing blue eyes aren't icy anymore. They are wide, filled with a raw, agonizing conflict.

"You shouldn't be out here, Clara," he says. His voice cuts through the thunder effortlessly.

"Neither should you!" I shout back, stepping closer, trying to shield him with the useless umbrella. "You're freezing! What are you doing standing in my yard?"

"I'm not cold," he murmurs.

To prove it, he reaches out. His large hand hovers near my wet cheek, his fingers brushing against a stray strand of my hair. The moment his skin makes contact, a gasp catches in my throat. He is radiating a shocking, impossible heat—like a roaring hearth in the middle of a blizzard.

He stares down at me, his thumb gently tracing my jawline. The awkward, brooding boy from the library completely vanishes, replaced by someone intensely present, looking at me with a depth of emotion that leaves me utterly breathless.

"I've spent a very long time avoiding people," Gideon says softly, his blue eyes searching mine. "It's safer that way. For everyone. But when you're in the room... I can't look away. I *shouldn't* be looking, Clara. But I am."

My heart hammers violently against my ribs. "Gideon, what are you talking about? What is happening on that ridge?"

At the mention of the ridge, the warmth in his expression shatters. He pulls his hand back, the sudden loss of his heat making me shiver against the rain. He looks back toward the woods, his jaw clenching.

"A storm is coming," he says, his voice dropping to a grave, urgent whisper. "Not just this rain. Something old, and something cruel. You need to take your family and leave Dinwiddie, Clara. Please."

Before I can demand an answer, he steps backward into the brush. The leaves rustle, the shadows of the storm swallow him up, and just like that, he is gone.

By Monday morning, the rain has stopped, but the heavy, expectant weight in the air remains. I sit in fifth-period art class, my brain entirely short-circuited as I try to process the impossible heat of Gideon's skin and his desperate warning. He wasn't at school today, something I did not expect to feel so sad about.

Across the wooden table, Bree is practically vibrating with excitement, helping Rowan mix a vibrant palette of acrylic paints.

"I'm telling you, Ro, it's going to be so romantic," Bree gushes, her bouncy blonde ponytail swaying. "Pip promised to take me up to the old Civil War earthworks on the ridge tonight to watch the sunset. He said there's a spot where you can see the whole valley."

"Bree, I told you, the ridge isn't safe right now," Rowan says, her voice low and grounding as she sets her paintbrush down. She glances at me, her dark eyes filled with worry. "The energy up there is wrong."

"Oh, come on, I'll be with Pip! What's going to happen?" Bree laughs it off, entirely oblivious.

While they talk, my charcoal pencil flies across my sketchbook, frantically trying to exhale the images trapped in my head. I shade the broad shoulders, the sharp jawline, the piercing eyes. I'm so lost in the drawing that I don't realize what I've actually created until Rowan suddenly gasps, stepping closer to my stool.

"Clara..." Rowan whispers, her face going stark pale. "Where did you see that?"

I blink, pulling myself out of the trance to look down at my page.

I had drawn Gideon. But I hadn't drawn him in his flannel jacket or his school clothes. Unconsciously, my hand had meticulously detailed a heavy, frayed woolen coat—a historically accurate Union army uniform jacket. Right down to the specific, tarnished brass buttons and the infantry insignia on the collar.

"I... I don't know," I stammer, my throat going dry. "I just... it's just what came to mind."

Rowan looks from the drawing to me, her voice dropping to a terrified whisper. "Clara, that's a 160-year-old uniform. Why would your mind put him in *that*?"

Suddenly, the puzzle pieces slam together in my brain with a force that makes my dizzy.

The perfect, military-style flinch at the loud noise in the library. Pip's slip-up about the mud in 'that April.' The impossible, burning heat of Gideon's skin in the freezing rain. The old family name that owns the ridge.

They aren't just an old family. They've been here the whole time.

The loud, metallic buzz of the school bell rings, signaling

the end of the day. Bree grabs her bag with a cheerful wave. "See you guys tomorrow!" she calls out, heading for the door. Rowan decided to walk home with me today. I wanted to know more about how she was feeling since she's always so worried about the ridge. We stopped by an old magnolia tree.

My fingers fiddled with the drawing of Gideon in my pocket. Ro' was mid sentence about the clay here having healing powers, and how it helped drive the evil out in 1865 when suddenly panic spikes through my chest. I rip out my drawing of the Union soldier uniform, and immediately Gideon's warning echoes in my ears: *Something old, and something cruel.*

And Bree is heading straight into those woods.

EIGHT

The trek through the woods is a grueling race against the fading twilight. The humidity of the afternoon has curdled into a suffocating, breathless heat, and the shadows of the Virginia pines stretch long, and jagged across the overgrown path. Beside me, Rowan moves with an intense, quiet focus, her hand occasionally brushing against the pocket of her jacket where I know she keeps her family's herbal mixtures.

"We're close," Rowan breathes, her dark eyes scanning the dense canopy. "There's an old, two-story brick building just past the main battlefield clearing. It was an officers' headquarters in 1865. Pip's family manages the preservation site, so he would have the keys to the upper observation deck."

As if on cue, the dense treeline suddenly breaks open, revealing a sweeping, tragic landscape. The historic battlefield is a massive clearing of high, golden grass, cut in half by deep, crumbling dirt trenches. Sitting on a knoll overlooking the valley is the building. A weathered, red-brick structure with boarded-up first floor windows and a wrap around wooden balcony on the second floor.

Up on that balcony, two figures are silhouetted against a bruised, blood-orange sunset.

"Bree!" I gasp, stepping forward, but Rowan catches my arm, her grip tight.

"Wait," she whispers, her eyes locked on the edge of the woods closest to the house. "Look."

The twilight air suddenly feels freezing, stripping away the summer heat in a single, unnatural breath. The sweet scent of the pine trees instantly replaced by a smell that makes my stomach turn—it reeks of ancient dust, and old copper.

A man steps out from the shadow of a massive oak tree near the brick building.

He doesn't look like a monster. He wears a dark tailored suit that looks entirely modern. I watched him take a few strides, and there is something deeply wrong with the way he moves. It's completely unnerving. It's too smooth, too perfect, like a predator mimicking human posture. His hair is slicked back, and even from this distance his presence radiates as menacing.

Up on the balcony, Pip suddenly tenses. I watch him step in front of Bree, his posture shifting from a relaxed teenager on a date to a rigid, protective soldier.

"Who's there?" Pip's voice echoes down from the balcony, lacking any of his usual playful charm. "The park is closed to the public."

The man in the suit doesn't answer. He simply walks forward, his shoes making no sound against the gravel, and as he inched closer Pip threw himself off the balcony with terrifying speed.

"Hey! Back off!" Pip shouts.

Before Bree can even scream, the man moves like a blur of darkness. He lashes out, his hand gripping Pip by the throat and slamming him hard against the brick wall of the building. The impact is so violent the old wood of the balcony rattles.

"Pip!" Bree shrieks, backing away into the corner.

"Still hiding in the skin of a boy, Caleb?" the man purrs, his voice a smooth, cultured baritone that carries effortlessly across the clearing. "Let me see what is underneath. Let me see my soldier."

The man raises a heavy silver cane, the tip carved into a jagged geometric shape, and strikes Pip hard across the chest.

Pip lets out a raw, agonized roar—a sound that starts human but rapidly drops into a deep, guttural, animalistic chest-rumble that shakes the very air. For a terrifying second, Pip's silhouette seems to expand, his shoulders widening, his hands curling into massive, shadowed claws as the ancient curse inside him fights to break through his human form.

"He's trying to force the transformation!" Rowan screeches to me, her voice laced with panic. "If he changes in front of Bree—"

"Hey!" I scream at the top of my lungs, adrenaline completely overriding my fear.

I break away from Rowan, sprinting out of the treeline and into the open battlefield clearing, holding my heavy sketchbook up like a weapon. "Get away from them!"

Rowan steps out right behind me, her hands raised, chanting a low, rhythmic sequence of words in a language that seems to make the surrounding pine trees rustle in defiance. She pulls a handful of dried, crushed herbs from her pocket and hurls them into the air, the wind catching the dust and sweeping it toward the balcony in a sudden, blinding cloud of green and silver.

The Occultist pauses, his hand still gripping Pip's shirt. He turns his head slowly, his cold, dead eyes locking onto me, then shifting to Rowan. A look of mild annoyance crosses his aristocratic features. He looks at the two of us, then back at Pip, who is slouched against the wall, panting heavily as his body painfully forces itself back into a normal human shape.

The man realizes he is outnumbered in the open, the element of surprise entirely gone.

"An interesting defense," the Occultist says smoothly, adjusting his cuffs as if he hadn't just tried to summon a monster. He steps back toward the balcony stairs, his eyes lingering on me with a terrifying, calculating curiosity. "We will finish our inspection later, Caleb. Enjoy your sunset."

In a blink, he slips back into the deep shadows, vanishing into the woods before the dust from Rowan's herbs can even settle on the ground around us.

I don't waste a second. I sprint up the wooden stairs, my lungs burning, with Rowan hot on my heels.

We burst onto the balcony. Bree is hyperventilating, collapsed on the floor with her face buried in her hands, sobbing uncontrollably. Pip is slumped against the brick wall, clutching his chest where the cane had struck him. His skin is burning hot. And holy smokes there is steam literally rising from his clothes into the cool night air. Pips eyes... usually so warm are wide with a feral, lingering panic. Leaving Rowan to tend to Bree I go to him.

He looks up at me, his jaw trembling. "Clara... he's back." I break his gaze to look back up to Rowan, as she's trying to get Bree to settle.

"Bree, look at me. Look at my eyes, you're safe," she pleads, her hands shaking as she leads her away from the corner of the balcony.

She is hyperventilating, her fingers clawing into the fabric of her varsity cheerleader jacket. Her eyes are wild, staring blankly at the dark woods where the man in the suit had just dissolved. "He… he had a weird cane," she chokes out, her voice cracking into a sob. "He just came out of nowhere, He hit Pip. Did you hear that sound Pip made? It sounded like… like a car engine blowing up. I thought he was going to die." She makes her way to us dropping down to him on weak knees. Her entire body is vibrating from terror.

Pip is slouched against the weathered red brick, his head between his knees. He is trying to stifle a deep, ragged wheeze that still sounds entirely too low, too hollow to belong to a human chest. I can see the air shimmering around him. The cool evening mist is turning to steam the second it hits his skin.

Rowan kneels beside him, entirely focused. She pulls a small glass vial filled with a dark, greenish fluid from her pocket, a thick herbal tincture.

"Drink this, Caleb. Now," Rowan commands, her voice a steady, grounding anchor.

Pip grabs the vial with a hand that still looks slightly too large, his fingernails jagged and thick. He gulps it down. Within seconds, a long, shuddering breath escapes him, and the unnatural heat radiating from his body begins to recede. He looks up at me, the lingering pale green in his irises slowly bleeding back into a normal, deep mossy hue.

"We have to get her out of here," Pip rasps, nodding weakly toward Bree. "Before he comes back."

"Can you walk?" I ask, wrapping an arm around Bree's waist to help her stand.

"I'll take him," a deep, quiet voice calls out from the base of the wooden stairs.

EIGHT

I flinch, spinning around. Silas Vance steps out from the shadows on the edge of the battlefield. He moves with that same impossible, eerie silence. He doesn't look surprised by the blood-orange sky, the crying girl, or the steaming boy. He just scales the distance in three massive strides, slinging Pip's arm over his broad shoulders without a word.

"Take Bree home," Silas tells me, his dark eyes dead serious. "We'll handle the rest." I dart my eyes to another figure standing in the distance… the unforgettable silhouette of one Gideon Beaumont.

The walk back down the ridge was filled with a smothering vastness of trees followed by Bree's quiet, rhythmic sobbing. She has completely rationalized the horror. By the time we get to her driveway, she's convinced herself that they were just assaulted by an unhinged local hiding out in the state park, and that Pip had simply screamed out in agonizing pain.

"Don't tell my mom," Bree begs, wiping her eyes as she grips the door handle. "Please, Clara. If she thinks the ridge is dangerous, she'll make me quit the squad. She'll never let me see Pip again."

I look at her bright, innocent face, a horrible weight settling in the pit of my stomach. "I won't say anything, Bree. Just go lock your doors. Get some sleep."

The second her front door clicks shut, I turn to Rowan, who has been quiet the entire trip back…. "We aren't going home, are we?" I ask. My heart pounding against my ribs.

Rowan meets my gaze, her face illuminated by the moonlight. "No. It's time we get our answers."

A cold shiver washes over me, chasing away the lingering warmth of the walk back down the ridge. I look from Rowan's fiercely determined eyes back to Bree's house, where a single porch light flickers, completely oblivious to the shifting reality we've just been dragged into.

"Answers," I repeat, the word heavy and foreign on my tongue. "From Gideon? Rowan, you saw what happened up there. Whatever they are keeping from us, it isn't just a regular secret. It's dangerous."

"Exactly," Rowan says, her voice dropping to a sharp, quiet whisper as she turns away from the driveway and begins marching down the dark asphalt. "Which is why we can't sit around waiting for them to decide when we're allowed to know the truth. Pip is hurt, Bree is terrified out of her mind, and you and I are right in the middle of it. I'm not going home to hide under my covers and pretend tonight didn't happen."

I sprint a few steps to catch up with her, my sneakers crunching loudly against the loose gravel at the edge of the road. The night air feels heavy, pressing against my chest as my heart continues its erratic, frantic rhythm. The shadows cast by the overhanging trees seem longer now, stretching across the path like grasping fingers. Every rustle of the wind through the leaves makes me flinch, my mind replaying Pip's agonizing scream on a terrifying loop.

We walk in a tense, suffocating silence, leaving the safety of the residential street behind. The town fades into darkness, swallowed by the looming woods that border the massive, iron-gated properties on the edge of the town. Rowan doesn't look back once. Her shoulders are set, her hands shoved deep into her jacket pockets, driving us forward with a terrifying momentum.

I know exactly where she's taking us. The sprawling, historic grounds have always cast a long shadow over this town, but tonight, the thought of walking up to those massive front doors makes my stomach twist into painful knots. We are stepping into the lion's den, entirely unprepared for whatever truth is waiting for us behind those walls.

As the paved road gives way to the winding, gravel path that cuts through the thick perimeter of forest, the towering silhouette of our destination finally begins to rise against the backdrop of the trees.

NINE

The Beaumont estate sits so deep into the foothills of the ridge line that the dense Virginia canopy completely swallows the moon. It's a massive, ancient property constructed from dark, jagged river stone, looking more like an 1800s fortress than a modern home.

Rowan doesn't knock. She pushes the heavy oak front door open, and we step into a room that feels entirely frozen in time.

There are no modern television screens or bright lights. A massive stone hearth dominates the back wall, a roaring fire casting long, dancing shadows across heavy velvet chairs, iron light fixtures, and walls lined with yellowed maps.

On a long leather sofa, Pip is stretched out, his shirt off, exposing a terrifying, deep purple bruise across his ribs in the exact shape of a geometric ward. Silas is quietly pressing a cloth soaked in a pungent, herbal poultice against the wound.

NINE

But it's the figure pacing in front of the hearth that commands the room.

Gideon.

The moment the door clicks behind us, he snaps his head around. He isn't the quiet, brooding boy from English class anymore. His posture is rigid, his broad shoulders tense, and his piercing blue eyes are burning with a raw, volatile mix of fury and terror.

"What were you thinking?" Gideon roars, his deep voice rattling the glass panes of the windows. He storms across the room, stopping mere inches from me. The sheer presence of him is suffocating, and that impossible, wild scent of sandalwood and sage fills my lungs. It's the same familiar smell I remember from my room the first night I came to town. His thundering voice cuts through my memory with a sharp sting. "I told you to stay away from the ridge, Clara! I told you to take your family and leave town!"

"I'm not going anywhere!" I shout back, matching his volume, my adrenaline completely overriding my fear. I rip my backpack off my shoulder, unzip it violently, and slam my sketchbook onto the wooden table between us.

I flip the page to the drawing of the him dressed as the Union soldier.

"Explain this, Gideon," I hiss, my finger tapping hard against the meticulously detailed 1865 uniform coat, the brass buttons, the infantry insignia. "Explain why Pip's skin was literally boiling tonight. Explain why you three flinch at loud noises like you're waiting for an artillery shell to drop, and why Pip talks about the mud in 1865 like he walked through it this morning!"

A heavy, suffocating silence drops over the room. The only sound is the crackle of the fireplace.

Gideon stares down at my drawing. The anger drains from his face, replaced by a profound, ancient exhaustion that makes him look entirely older than eighteen. He traces a large, calloused thumb over the charcoal lines of the uniform jacket.

"You really do have a gift," Gideon murmurs, his voice dropping to that low, tectonic rumble. "Your mind sees the truth before you even process it."

He looks up, those icy blue eyes locking onto mine with an intensity that pins me to the spot.

"We didn't grow up on this ridge, Clara," Gideon says softly. "We were Union soldiers of the 1865 campaign. We were dying on that battlefield when *he* found us."

"The man with the cane," I whisper, my breath catching in my throat.

"Magnus Pendleton," Silas chimes in from the sofa, his voice grim. "Or whatever name he's using in this century. He's an occultist. A shadow weaver. He used a corrupted, ancient blood magic to sew the spirits of the wild into our veins while our hearts were stopping. He wanted an army of unyielding, unstoppable beasts to turn the tide of the war."

"We broke free," Pip groans, wincing as Silas presses the poultice harder against his chest. "We used a ward made of native mud crafted by Rowan's ancestors to drive him out of our territory. But the magic bound us to the land. We became the guardians of the ridge. The 'monsters' the town folks whisper about." Silas whispers with a softness I have never heard him use.

My mind spins, the sheer impossibility of it crashing over me. They aren't teenagers. They are immortals carrying a centuries-old curse, living a double life to keep a monster sealed away.

Gideon steps even closer to me, cutting off my view of the

rest of the room. He reaches out, his large hand hovering just a millimeter away from my arm, the impossible, comforting heat of his skin radiating through my clothes.

"When we saw him tonight, he was testing Pip. He's trying to wake the beast up so he can retake control," Gideon says, his blue eyes searching mine. They were suddenly filled with a devastating vulnerability. "But when you and Rowan stepped out... you changed the game. He saw your face, Clara. He knows you're connected to us now."

"I'm not afraid of him," I say, though my voice trembles slightly.

"You should be," Gideon whispers, his hand finally closing gently over mine. His grip is firm, warm, and entirely protective.

"Because I've spent one hundred and sixty years with nothing to lose. But looking at you right now... I know he has a weapon to use against me."

Leaving the Beaumont house felt like I got more questions than answers. The phantom warmth of Gideon's hand lingered on my skin long after he let go. It was a sharp contrast to the biting night air that hit us the moment we stepped off the porch.

Beside me, Rowan walked in a tense, brooding silence, her boots clicking sharply against the pavement. The weight of Gideon's words hung heavily between us. *He has a weapon to use against me*. The thought sent chills straight down my spine, and they had nothing to do with the weather.

"We need to get inside," Rowan said quietly, her eyes scanning the shadows of the tree-lined street. "You're staying at my place tonight. If he knows you're connected to them, I'm not letting you out of my sight."

I didn't argue. The sheer exhaustion of the night was finally catching up to me, pulling at my limbs. "What about the boys?"

"I already texted them," Rowan replied, pulling her jacket tighter against the wind. "They're laying low tonight, but we're meeting them at my apothecary first thing in the morning. We'll figure out a plan then. For now, we just need to make it through the night."

I took one last glance back at the looming silhouette of the Beaumont house, its dark windows staring back like empty eye sockets. Gideon was right... the game had changed. Sleep would be hard to come by tonight, but as we hurried toward Rowan's house, I knew the morning would bring a confrontation we couldn't run from.

TEN

The next morning I rush out the door with Rowan. Our sleepover did not provide any sleep. We spent the entire night searching books from Rowan's family history for any clues on how to fight Pendleton.

We make our way to the apothecary, once inside I noticed the vibes feel different today. The boys are already inside waiting for us. The comforting scents of lavender, and sage are still there lingering in the air, but they are buried beneath the sharp, metallic tang of iron and sulfur. Thick bundles of roots hang from the wooden rafters, casting long, skeletal shadows across the counter where the old leather-bound journal from 1865 lies wide open.

"The magic Pendleton used wasn't just a spell," Rowan says, her voice low as she crushes dried leaves into a stone mortar. The pestle grinds with a rhythmic, scraping sound. "It was a corruption of the land's natural defense. To fight him, we have to anchor the boys' humanity before they face him, or he'll pull the beast right out of them."

She hands a steaming iron mug to Pip, who is sitting on a wooden stool, still clutching his bruised ribs. The liquid inside is thick, dark, and smells faintly of woodsmoke.

Pip winces, taking a swallow. Almost instantly, a shudder ripples through his frame. His eyes flash a violent, untamed before bleeding back to normal. A thin layer of sweat breaking out across his forehead. “It burns,” he rasps, leaning his head against the brick wall. “But… the roar in my head is quieter. It feels further away.”

Silas stands by the back door, arms crossed like a sentinel, watching the woods. “Good. Because when the storm hits, we can’t afford a lapse in control.”

In the corner of the room, Gideon sits at a heavy oak table right next to me. His shoulder is pressed against mine. His intense, burning heat a constant grounding presence. Spread between us are three fresh pages from my sketchbook.

“Look at the lines Clara,” Gideon murmurs. His deep baritone brushing against my ear sends chills down my spine. His large, calloused hand hovers over the jagged geometric pattern I had mindlessly traced under the magnolia tree when we stopped on the walk over this morning.

“You didn’t just draw a symbol. Look at the corners. Those are topographical coordinates. Your hand is mapping the weak points in the ridge line seal.”

I trace my fingers over the charcoal. It’s terrifyingly true. What I thought was abstract shading is actually a flawless layout of the old Civil War earthworks. “My mind is drawing where he’s going to strike next,” I whisper.

Gideon’s hand slides over mine, his grip firm and desperate. “Which means we use it to strike first. Rowan has a ritual to reinforce the ward at the old officers’ quarters. Silas, Pip, and I will draw Pendleton out into the open battlefield. We destroy him there."

"And what about Bree?" I ask, my heart tightening with an anxious panic.

"She's safe," Gideon says fiercely, his piercing eyes locking onto mine, filled with protective focus. "Silas checked the schedule. She has the varsity pep rally at the high school stadium friday night. She'll be surrounded by hundreds of people, bright lights, and coaches. Pendleton can't touch her in a crowd. It keeps her entirely clear of the ridge."

I look down at our joined hands, feeling the impossible fire radiating from his skin. For a fleeting moment, surrounded by the scent of Rowan's herbs and the steady weight of Gideon's presence, I actually believe we can win. I feel a quiet, beautiful spark of hope.

"We do this together," I tell him.

Gideon doesn't answer with words. He brings my hand up to his lips, his warm breath brushing against my knuckles as he presses a soft, lingering kiss to my skin. "Together," he promises softly.

Outside the frosted glass of the apothecary window, the first heavy rumble of thunder rattles the frames. The sky is turning a violent, bruised purple. The plan is set, and the trap is laid. We gathered our things in silence, stepping out into the unknown.

The air outside is thick and electric. Gideon stays close, his shoulder a solid, grounding weight against mine as the first fat drops of rain begin to splatter against the pavement. Across the street, Silas is already waiting by the truck, his expression as dark and unreadable as the storm clouds rolling over the ridge.

We don't speak on the ride back. There's nothing left to say. The pieces are on the board, the safety of a crowded Friday night stadium dangling ahead of us like a beacon. But as I watch the dark woods blur past the window, I can't shake the chilling realization of what lies between now and then.

When Gideon pulls the truck to a stop, he doesn't let me go without one last, lingering look. I head inside, locking the door behind me and leaning against it as the storm finally breaks overhead, unleashing a torrential downpour. I watch the lightning illuminate the kitchen in stark, ghostly flashes, wondering how a town that used to feel so safe can suddenly feel so vulnerable.

That night, I lie awake listening to the rain beat a relentless rhythm against the roof. The spark of hope Gideon gave me still burns, but it's a small flame against a vast, oncoming dark. I close my eyes, bracing myself for the agonizing stretch of days to come, praying that Pendleton stays blind to our trap.

When sleep finally takes me, it's restless and haunted by the shadow of the ridge.

ELEVEN

The week goes by in a blur. But, walking into school on Friday morning feels like stepping across a fault line. The fluorescent lights are bright, the linoleum floors scuffed, and the lockers loud. The world I lived in Monday has completely evaporated.

I feel my heart doing a nervous little dance against my ribs. Gideon grabs my hand, leading me to our empty seats in the back.

He doesn't avoid my gaze this time. As I sit down, his piercing blue eyes lock onto mine, intense and unyielding. He still has that commanding presence that makes the room feel entirely too small. The icy barrier between us is gone. In its place is a heavy, quiet gravity.

We can't talk about Civil War curses, blood magic, or 160-year-old battlefields while Mr. Harrison stands at the chalkboard unrolling a map of Virginia. But the silence between us isn't empty anymore; it's electric.

When Mr. Harrison passes back our project rubrics, Gideon reaches out to take the papers. Our hands brush. The moment his fingers touch my skin, that impossible spark surges through me, chasing away the chill clinging to stagnant air. He lingers for just a fraction of a second, his gaze dropping to my lips before he pulls away. My breath hitches, and I have to stare down at my notebook just to remind myself how to breathe.

He isn't pulling back to protect his secret anymore. He's standing guard.

By lunchtime, for the first time since I moved to Dinwiddie, the table in the corner of the cafeteria isn't just Bree, and Rowan, and I. Silas, and Pip walk out of the lunch line and slide into the empty seats next to us. Silas sits like a boulder, his dark eyes casually scanning the crowded room, while Pip gingerly adjusts his posture, a faint wince crossing his face as he guards his bruised ribs.

Then comes Gideon. He takes the seat right next to me, his broad shoulder pressing lightly against mine, anchoring me to the spot.

To anyone else in the cafeteria, we just look like a sudden, eclectic group of friends. The cheerleader, the artsy new girl, the quiet herbalist, and the three rugged guys who live up on the ridge. But beneath the table, the energy is vibrating like a live wire.

"I'm telling you guys, I'm totally fine," Bree says, her voice a little too high, a little too fast as she mindlessly picks at her salad. Her signature bouncy blonde ponytail is swept up, but the dark circles under her eyes tell the real story. She hasn't slept. "It was just some creepy guy in a suit. A transient or something. Pip's family is going to report it to the county historical society."

"Exactly, Bree-Bree," Pip chimes in, forcing a charming, easygoing smile that doesn't quite reach his eyes. He reaches across the table, his hand wrapping over hers. "Just a freak incident. We aren't going back up to the ruins anyway. It's boring up there."

Silas nods once, his voice a low, gravelly rasp. "Town is safer."

I watch Bree let out a long, shuddering sigh of relief, completely melting into the lie. She has no idea that the three boys sitting with her are ancient guardians, or that Rowan is tracking shifting shadows. She doesn't know that we aren't just eating lunch. We are acting as a human shield, burying her in the middle of a fortress so the man with the silver cane can't get a clear shot.

Gideon's hand shifts under the table, his large, warm fingers finding mine in the hidden space between our chairs. He squeezes gently, his skin radiating that fierce, protective heat. I look up, meeting his icy blue eyes, and the sheer weight of his devotion hits me like a physical wave.

We are keeping her safe. We are keeping each other safe.

But as I look past Gideon's shoulder toward the large glass windows of the cafeteria, watching the dark, jagged pine trees of the ridge line sway against a bruised sky, a shiver cuts right through his warmth.

The shield is holding for now. But out there in the woods, the storm is waiting.

Around us, the mundane noise of the high school cafeteria goes on completely uninterrupted. Trays clatter into metal racks, laughter erupts from a nearby table, and someone drops a water bottle that clangs loudly against the linoleum. Bree reaches for her sandwich, chatting about the pep rally, entirely insulated by our presence. She doesn't notice how Rowan's gaze constantly tracks the perimeter of the room, or how Silas sits perfectly rigid, his muscles coiled like a spring.

Gideon's thumb rubs a slow, reassuring circle against the back of my hand under the table. It's a silent lifeline, keeping me anchored while my mind races ahead to the coming hours. We just have to keep the illusion alive until tonight.

When the bell finally rings, signaling the end of lunch, the sudden movement of hundreds of students feels like a tactical shift. We stand in unison, automatically forming a loose perimeter around Bree as we blend into the crowded hallway. Gideon gives my hand one last squeeze before releasing it, his reassuring eyes locking onto mine with a look that says everything his lips can't.

By day, we play our parts flawlessly. We walk the halls, and maintain the fragile fiction that everything is normal. I sit through lectures with a racing pulse, staring out classroom windows at the ominous, shifting shadows of the ridge. Every time a door slams too loudly or footsteps echo in an empty corridor, my heart leaps into my throat, half-expecting to see the glint of a silver cane. But Pendleton stays in the dark, watching from a distance, completely unaware that his targets are quietly weaving a net of their own.

By night, the atmosphere in the apothecary shifts from a sanctuary to a war room. We gather under the dim, amber lights. The blue prints of the quarters are spread across the wooden table, the edges weighed down by jars of protective charms.

We check every angle, debate every variable, and rehearse our movements until they are second nature. The pressure is immense, a heavy suffocating weight that grows with each passing minute. We are exhausted, operating on frayed nerves and pure adrenaline, but the fierce devotion holding us together never waivers.

As the final preparations are made, Rowan seals the last of

the tracking charms with a quiet incantation. Gideon stands by the window, staring out into the night toward the ridge, his silhouette imposing and resolute. The time for waiting is over. The pieces are finally on the board.

TWELVE

The storm doesn't just break over the ridge; it tears it open. Rain lashes the high, golden grass of the battlefield clearing, turning the deep Civil War trenches into rushing rivers of red Virginia clay.

Standing on the second-floor wooden balcony of the brick officers' quarters, I pull my jacket tight against the freezing wind. Beside me, Rowan is tracing a final, glowing silver line of crushed iron-weed along the door frame. The ancient geometric ward from my sketchbook is finally complete, etched into the threshold of the historic lookout.

"The seal is set," Rowan yells over the howling wind, her dark eyes flashing in the lightning. "If we can force him across this line, the blood bond will lock. He won't be able to dissolve or flee."

Down in the muddy clearing below, the trap springs itself.

A lone figure steps out from the lashing treeline. Arthur Pendleton moves with a terrifying, unhurried grace. His dark tailored suit is completely untouched by the torrential downpour. He holds his heavy silver cane loosely at his side, his cold, aristocratic eyes fixed on the house.

"You call for me, Caleb?" Pendleton's smooth baritone cuts through the thunder effortlessly. "I see you brought your brothers-in-arms this time."

With a deafening roar that starts in a human throat but rapidly drops into a guttural, earth-shaking rumble, Gideon, Silas, and Pip explode from the shadows of the trenches.

For the first time, I see what they truly are.

They don't fully change into monsters, but the humanity drains from them in an instant. Gideon's shoulders expand to an impossible breadth, his fingers lengthening into thick, shadowed talons. His jaw squares, and his piercing blue eyes ignite into a wild, blazing amber that outshines the lightning. He moves with a supernatural speed, throwing his massive frame directly at the Occultist.

The collision sounds like a cannon fire echoing across the valley.

Gideon strikes Pendleton, driving him back into the mud. Silas closes in from the flank, his arms shifting with thick, dark fur as he unleashes a Feral swipe that splinters the trunk of a nearby pine. Pip arcs around the rear, his teeth bared in a razor-sharp snarl, his movements completely unbothered by the bruised ribs he carried just hours ago.

They are fighting with the synchronized precision of an elite military unit—soldiers who have shared a blood bond for a hundred and sixty years.

"Now, Gideon! Force him toward the stairs!" I scream from the balcony, gripping the wooden railing so hard my knuckles turn white.

Gideon grabs Pendleton by the lapels of his suit, his massive clawed hands radiating a fierce, steaming heat in the downpour. With a surge of pure cryptid strength, he hurls the Occultist through the air. Pendleton crashes against the wooden stairs, coughing up dark, thick blood. He looks up at the balcony, his sharp jaw clenching as he realizes he is entirely outnumbered, trapped between three ancient guardians and a binding ward.

But he doesn't look afraid.

Slowly, a chilling, cruel smile spreads across his smug features. He wipes the blood from his lip with a pristine cufflink. Turning to Gideon, he gives a deep chuckle.

"An excellent ambush, Major Beaumont," Pendleton purrs, his voice dripping with venomous amusement. "You've trained your new little scouts well. But tell me… who is guarding the stadium?" And with a seething huff he vanishes into thin air.

My blood turns to absolute ice.

The space where Pendleton had been standing a micro-second before is entirely empty, save for a lingering wisp of black oily smoke instantly shredded by the torrential downpour. The heavy rumble of thunder echoes overhead, mocking the sudden, sickening silence that descends on the stairs.

"No!" Pip barks, lunging forward, his hands outstretched as if he could physically tear the occultist back from whatever shadows he just slipped through. He drops to his knees on the wet wooden steps, his fingers brushing the spot where Pendleton had coughed up dark, thick blood. The binding ward we spent days preparing flickers wildly, its glowing lines sputtering and dying out like a spent match. "He bypassed it. How the hell did he bypass it?"

Gideon doesn't answer. He stands frozen, his massive clawed hands still smoking in the rain, his chest heaving with a mixture of spent cryptid strength and rising fury. His icy blue eyes stare blankly at the empty space, the fierce, protective heat that usually radiates from him turning into a terrifying aura.

"The stadium," Silas says, his voice cutting through the rain like a razor. He steps out from the shadows of the balcony. His usual calculated calm is now entirely shattered. His jaw is clenched so tight I can hear his teeth grind. "He was a distraction. The whole thing. He wanted us here, away from her."

The realization hits me like a physical blow, knocking the breath straight out of my lungs. *The pep rally.* We thought we were burying Bree in a fortress of bright lights and hundreds of people. We thought a crowded stadium kept her entirely clear of the ridge. But Pendleton didn't care about the crowd. We had left her completely vulnerable.

THIRTEEN

A sudden vibration rattles against my ribs.

I fumble with my wet pockets, my trembling fingers pulling out my phone. The screen is smeared with rainwater, but the bright notification cuts through the darkness like a blade. It's from Bree's phone.

My heart stops. It's not a text. It's a photo.

The image is blurry, taken in the lashing rain at the dark edge of the high school football field. There, laid out in the muddy grass is Bree's bright varsity cheerleader jacket discarded. Next to it, glinting under the distant stadium lights, is her silver charm bracelet.

"No," I choke out, the phone slipping from my hand and clattering against the balcony floorboards. "No, no, no."

"Clara?" Rowan gasps, rushing to my side.

Down in the mud, Gideon hears my cry. He snaps his head up, his blazing amber eyes widening as he reads the pure horror on my face. Then all in an instant, a bright flash appears. He has returned. In that split second of distraction, Pendleton strikes. He drives the silver tip of his cane into Gideon's chest, the geometric carving flaring with a blinding, purple spark of blood magic.

Gideon roars in agony, collapsing into the mud as the steam violently rushes from his skin.

"You thought a crowd would stop me?" Pendleton laughs, his voice echoing over the thunder as he steps back into the safety of the dark treeline. "I built the shadows of this ridge, children. A few stadium lights are nothing to me. Oh, and thank you for clearing the forest. It gave us the privacy we required. Such a sweet girl, that Bree."

"Gideon!" I shriek, sprinting down the wooden stairs, completely ignoring the mud lashing at my jeans.

By the time Silas and Pip pull Gideon to his feet, his amber eyes are fading back to a fractured, exhausted blue. The Occultist is gone. The clearing is empty. The trap turned out to be a perfectly devastating diversion.

"We have to go," Pip rasps, his voice trembling with a terror I've never heard from him before. "We have to get back to the school."

The raw, panic in his eyes makes my stomach violently twist. "We need to get to the truck. Now."

We break into a frantic sprint, splashing blindly through the mud and the dark. The pouring rain blinds me, stinging my eyes and soaking through my clothes, but I barely feel it. The only thing I can hear over the howling wind is the rhythmic, terrifying echo of Pendleton's last words looping in my head: *Who is guarding the stadium?*

We pile into the truck in a chaotic rush of slamming doors and heavy breathing. Silas throws the vehicle into reverse, the tires spinning and spitting gravel before catching onto the main road. The headlights cut thin, weak beams through the wall of water ahead of us. Nobody speaks. The air inside the cabin is thick, suffocating, and heavy with the terrifying scent of our own failure.

I pull my knees to my chest, staring out the passenger window into the pitch-black night, my whole body shaking uncontrollably. I clamp my jaw shut to keep my teeth from chattering. *Please be okay,* I pray silently into the dark, my heart hammering against my ribs like a trapped bird. *Please, Bree, just be okay.*

I reach into my pocket, my slick, wet fingers wrap tightly around my phone. The drive back to town was a frantic, silent blur of spinning tires and blinding rain. We don't even make it to the stadium parking lot. Halfway down the access road bordering woods behind the school, Silas slams on the brakes.

The headlights cut through the torrential sheets of water, illuminating the edge of the tree line.

A figure is stumbling out from the brush.

"Bree!" I scream, throwing the passenger door open and throwing myself out into the storm.

She is disoriented. Her white cheer skirt is torn, and coated in dark forest mud. Her blonde hair plastered to her face. She walks with a strange, jerky, uncoordinated gait, her head tilted down toward the earth.

"Bree, oh my god, Bree, I'm so sorry," I sob, rushing forward to wrap my arms around her.

The moment my hands touch her shoulders, I freeze.

She isn't cold from the rain. Her skin is radiating an impossible, feverish heat—the exact same fire that lives in Gideon's veins.

Slowly, Bree raises her head.

The sweet, innocent girl who spent yesterday picking at salads and talking about Friday night football games is entirely gone. Her jaw is clenching so hard the bones are shifting, a low, terrified, whimper escaping her throat. And when she opens her eyes… the familiar, bright blue is completely buried.

They are glowing a terrifying, untamed amber.

She looks at Pip, then at me, her hands curling into tight, trembling fists as her fingernails begin to thicken and darken into jagged claws. The ancient blood magic has already taken hold.

The Occultist didn't abduct her to use her as bait. He turned her. He left her here as a message to the Calvary : *The new army has begun.*

Bree lets out a raw, agonizing screech that tears through the night air. Her body begins to expand painfully as she undergoes her very first transformation collapsing into the muddy grass at our feet.

FOURTEEN

The basement of the Beaumont fortress feels less like a home, and more like a cage tonight. The heavy river-stone walls are damp, and the only illumination comes from a few flickering iron lanterns that cast long, erratic shadows across the concrete floor.

In the center of the room, behind a hastily reinforced perimeter of heavy iron chains and the glowing silver dust of Rowan's binding wards, Bree is screaming.

It isn't a human sound anymore. It's a wet, guttural screech that tears at the throat, blending the terrified cries of a teenage girl with the raw, cavernous roar of the beast waking up in her blood. Her spine is painfully arching as thick, dark shadow-fur ripples across her shoulders.

"Bree-Bree, please… look at me! Fight it!" Pip screams from the other side of the ward.

Silas has to hold him back, his thick arms wrapped around Pip's chest. Pip kicks, and thrashes as he watches a desperate Bree try to break through the chains holding her. Pip's face is tracked with tears, his amber eyes flaring as a reflection of his own absolute agony. "It's my fault," he chokes out, collapsing to his knees as Silas lowers him to the floor. "I brought her to the ruins. I let him see her. I did this to her."

"Caleb, stop," Silas says, his rough voice cracking with an uncharacteristic wave of emotion. "Pendleton was hunting. If it wasn't at the ridge, he would have taken her from her own bed. He wanted to break us. He wanted to show us we can't protect anything."

Across the room, Rowan is frantically flipping through her great-great-grandmother's 1865 journal, her hands trembling so hard a few loose dried leaves scatter across the floor. "There has to be a stabilizer. A tincture, a counter-spell, *something* to keep her mind intact before the beast swallows her completely."

"There isn't one, Rowan," Gideon's deep baritone cuts through the chaos.

He stands near the foot of the stairs, his broad frame cast entirely in shadow. His piercing blue eyes are dull, carrying a heavy, catastrophic weight. He looks at Bree's writhing form, then shifts his gaze to me.

"When Arthur turns someone, the first twenty-four hours are pure instinct," Gideon says softly, walking over to press his scorching-hot hand against my cold arm. The warmth is a lifeline in this freezing room, but his words are like ice. "If she breaks out of this basement tonight, she won't go home to her mother, Clara. She will hunt. And the town will do what a town does when they see a monster in the woods. They will track her down, and they will kill her."

I look through the iron chains at my best friend. The girl who asked for mani-pedi ideas yesterday is now clawing at the concrete, her wild amber eyes locked onto mine in a silent, terrified plea for help.

"We aren't going to let them touch her," I say. With a cold, unyielding resolve hardening in my chest, burning away the last of my tears, I look up at Gideon meeting his gaze fiercely. "We are going to hide her. We are going to protect her. And then, we are going to find a way to fix this."

Gideon stares at me for a long beat, the raw vulnerability in his eyes shifting into something lethal and fiercely devoted. "Whatever it takes, Clara," he whispers. "Whatever it takes."

The words hang in the freezing air of the basement, a solemn vow that binds us all to a terrifying new reality. Behind the heavy iron chains, a low growl vibrates from the shadows. I force myself not to flinch, keeping my eyes locked on the space where Bree—or the creature she is currently fighting against—is curled on the cold concrete. The sound is entirely feral, a sickening reminder of Gideon's warning. The girl who used to laugh in the school hallways is gone for now, replaced by an entity driven entirely by pure, predatory instinct.

Rowan steps forward quietly, the soft rustle of her jacket breaking the tense silence. She begins pulling jars from her pack, her hands steady despite the gravity of our situation. She sets up a perimeter of dried mountain ash and crushed wolfsbane along the base of the cell, murmuring a quiet, protective incantation under her breath to help mask her scent. Every time her fingers scatter the herbs, the creature behind the bars hisses, its amber eyes tracking her movements with dangerous focus.

Silas remains near the bottom of the wooden stairs, a silent, brooding sentinel. His arms are crossed over his chest, his eyes never leaving the reinforced door that leads up to the house. We all know what's at stake. If anyone from the town wanders out here, if a single person catches a glimpse of what Arthur has done to her, the countdown begins.

As the hours drag on, the basement becomes an endurance test of frayed nerves and suffocating dread. The storm outside reaches its peak, unleashing a relentless torrent against the small, dirt-streaked window near the ceiling. Loud cracks of thunder shake the very foundations of the house, rattling the iron bars and sending waves of dust down from the wooden rafters. Every sudden boom causes Bree to strike the concrete floor with her claws, a hollow, scraping sound that makes my chest ache.

Gideon doesn't leave my side. His grounding weight against my arm, providing the only source of warmth in the damp, freezing room. We sit together on a pair of overturned wooden crates, watching, waiting, and listening to the rhythmic sound of the pouring rain mixed with the restless shifting of our best friends.

Nobody sleeps. The night bleeds slowly into Saturday morning, marked only by the shifting gray light outside the high window. The initial frenzy of her transformation begins to give way to a heavy, exhausted stagnation, but the danger doesn't lessen. Gideon and Rowan take turns monitoring her vitals from a distance, noting the way the instinctual rage flares up whenever the wind howls too loudly against the house.

By Sunday, a profound, heavy silence settles over the room, broken only by the steady, muffled drumming of the rain. The adrenaline that kept us moving through the horror of the pep rally and the frantic chase has completely burned out, leaving behind a hollow, aching fatigue. We barely speak, exchanging only brief, whispered updates. We look at Bree, whose amber eyes occasionally soften into a dazed, confused look before the shadows take hold of her again.

I stare at my hands which have been shaking since this nightmare started. We are going to protect her, no matter how many days we have to spend in this dark, freezing cellar. We will hide her from the town, and we will find a way to break whatever hold Arthur has on her.

As the deep darkness of Sunday night closes in, the storm finally begins to lose its fury, the thunder echoing like a distant, dying threat over the ridge.

Wrapped in a heavy blanket with my head resting against Gideon's shoulder, I watch the shadows dance across the basement ceiling. I sit there waiting for the dawn of a new week, and the grueling battle we still have ahead of us.

FIFTEEN

By Monday morning, the storm had finally passed, leaving Dinwiddie bathed in a quiet, fragile sunlight that feels like a cruel joke. At school, the whispers have already begun. *Bree Miller didn't show up for homeroom. Her car is still in the student lot. Her mom filed a missing person's report over the weekend, and Bree's phone stopped sharing its location.*

I sit on the back porch of Nana's house, a cup of untouched tea cooling on the wooden table beside me. My sketchbook is propped on my knees. My fingers are stained black with charcoal, my hand moving across the paper in a frantic, feverish rhythm I can't seem to control.

The air behind me shifts, turning thick with the scent I know all too well.

I don't look up as Gideon steps onto the porch. He slides into the chair next to mine, his massive frame blocking out the cold wind. He doesn't say anything. He just reaches out, his warm hand settling over my knee, offering his silent, grounding strength.

"We managed to get her stabilized for now," Gideon says after a long silence, his voice is low. "Rowan brewed a sedative strong enough to quiet the roar in her head. She's sleeping. But it's temporary, Clara. Within a week, the moon will turn, and she will try to run to Pendleton. The creator's pull is too strong to resist."

"Then we have a week to find him," I say, my voice steady.

"We don't know where his main sanctuary is," Gideon mutters, his jaw clenching as he looks out toward the jagged, dark pine trees of the ridge line. "He's been hiding in the shadows of this valley for a century and a half. He only comes out when he wants to be seen."

"Gideon," I whisper, my breath catching in my throat as my charcoal pencil suddenly snaps against the paper. "Look."

I lift my hands away from the sketchbook.

During our conversation, my subconscious had taken over again. I had not drawn a uniform coat this time. I had drawn a map of the Civil War earthworks.

Spanned across the two-page layout is a terrifyingly detailed, sprawling underground cavern. Massive, jagged stalactites hang from a vaulted stone ceiling, and in the center of the cave is an ancient, crumbling brick foundation—the subterranean ruins of an antebellum plantation house buried deep beneath the mud.

But it's the center of the drawing that makes my heart hammer violently against my ribs.

Drawn in sharp, jagged lines is an ornate, dagger. The hilt is carved into the shape of a weeping crow with opal eyes, and the blade is etched with the exact same interlocking wards we tried to use to trap the Occultist on the balcony.

Beneath the weapon, I had scrawled a single line of text in

that same sweeping, old-fashioned cursive that I've only ever seen from one other person.

The blood that binds can bleed the weaver dry.

Gideon leans forward, his icy eyes widening as he stares at the page. His hand leaves my knee, his fingers trembling slightly as he touches the drawing of the iron dagger.

"The Crow-Hilt." Gideon breathes, his voice barely a whisper. He seems to be filled with a suddenly shocking spark of hope. "It's a relic from the 1865 campaign. Arthur's original focus. The Union army confiscated it before the battlefield campaign, but it was lost when the ridge line collapsed. If it's down in those caverns..."

"It can kill him." I finish the sentence for him, looking away from the drawing, and into his eyes. "It can break the blood bond."

Gideon looks at me, the quiet, protective boy completely vanishing, replaced by a leader who finally has a mission. He wraps his hands around mine, pulling me close until our foreheads touch, his breath hot against my lips.

"He thinks he won because he took Bree," Gideon whispers fiercely against my skin. "He has no idea that he left his map in your hands. We're going into the deep caverns, Clara. We're bringing that weapon back."

I close my sketchbook, the heavy thud of the cover sounding like a promise.

The battle for the ridge line was over. But the war for Dinwiddie had just begun.

A suffocating silence falls over the back porch of Nana's house, thick with the scent of damp earth and the chill of the midnight air. Gideon doesn't let go of my hands; his grip remains fierce, a desperate anchor in a world that has completely fractured around us. The rest of the house behind us is dark and still, the quiet of the night only amplifying the agonizing weight of our devastating defeat. But out here a cold, sharp resolve is finally beginning to solidify between the two of us.

"We don't have time on our side, Clara," Gideon says softly, his deep voice cutting straight through the dark. He looks down at the worn leather cover of my sketchbook, his eyes dark with an urgency that makes my chest tighten. "Rowan confirmed the timeline before she left. Bree's infection is accelerating. Arthur's curse isn't just sitting idle. We have seven days. Once the next full cycle hits a week from tonight, the transition becomes permanent. If we don't break Pendleton's hold before then, she will completely turn."

Seven days. The words echo like a death knell against my desperate ears. One week to navigate the treacherous, uncharted depths of the deep caverns where Pendleton thinks he has hidden his prize. One week to unearth an ancient relic, the only weapon capable of severing an occultist's binding contract. The only known blade sharp enough to pierce the supernatural shield Pendleton has built around himself.

Gideon draws my attention completely back to him, blocking out the rest of the world. The heat radiating from him is a fierce, tangible reminder of the ancient guardian strength flowing through his veins. Something wild countering the bitter night breeze. He looks down at me, his jaw set with an unyielding determination that scares me just as much as it comforts me.

"He thinks he's isolated us," Gideon murmurs, his voice dropping to a low vibration as his fingers tighten around mine. "He thinks because he took our shield, we'll back down. But we are going into his territory now. We play by our rules."

I squeeze his hands back. I want to be his constant, his

grounding light through all of this darkness.

The map is pressed safely inside the pages of my book. Pendleton has the power, and he has the resources. But he made one critical mistake: he left his blueprints in the hands of a group of friends who have absolutely nothing left to lose.

Outside, a sudden, violent gust of wind howls past the porch. It rustles the overgrown dark woods at the edge of the yard and causes the old wind chimes to clash like metal blades tracking our remaining time. Out there in the dark, hidden deep beneath the roots of the ancient forest, the caverns are waiting. Pendleton is waiting.

I take a deep, steadying breath, looking up into Gideon's fierce, devoted eyes. The final pieces are on the board, the countdown has officially begun, and a terrifying new path is unfolding beneath our feet. I pull him in, my lips brushing against his. For a moment, the cool beach waves my life had left behind flash before my eyes... Gideon brought me back to my happy place. I intend to do everything in my power to be his.

"Let's go hunt an occultist," I whisper into the dark.

A Sneak Peek at Book Two of the Midnight Calvary Trilogy...

'The blood that binds can bleed the weaver dry.'

-The surface of Dinwiddie is quiet, but beneath the historical town, an ancient darkness is breathing.

With only seven days before the turning of the moon, Clara and Gideon are running out of time. Bree is trapped in the depths of the Beaumont estate, fighting a losing battle against the feral curse roaring in her blood. Her only hope lies buried in the deep, uncharted caverns beneath the ridge line—a lost relic from the 1865 campaign known as the Crow-Hilt dagger.

But the underground ruins belong to Arthur Pendleton. And this time, he's waiting for them in the dark.

To save her best friend and break a century-old blood bond,

Clara will have to trust her prophetic sketches deeper than ever before. Guiding Gideon into a labyrinth of stone, shadows, and secrets that were meant to stay buried.

The rescue mission begins. But in the weaver's den, one wrong step means becoming part of his army forever.-

Coming Soon:

A DAGGER IN THE DEEP *Book Two of The Midnight Cavalry.*

Acknowledgments

Bringing *A Heart in the Trenches* to life has been a journey of passion, late nights, and profound transformation—both on the page and in my own life. This book would not exist without the incredible village of people who held me up, kept me inspired, and believed in my words when the world felt entirely overwhelming.

To my mother and my sister-in-law: thank you will never be enough. This year brought the greatest blessing of my life with the birth of my first child, but navigating early motherhood while trying to write a novel is a balancing act I couldn't have managed alone. Thank you for stepping in with endless love, for holding the baby so I could hold a pen, and for constantly reminding me to chase my dreams. Your unwavering support kept me focused, grounded, and inspired when I needed it most.

To my beautiful baby: you came into the world right alongside this story. Every word of this book was written with you in my arms or sleeping soundly nearby, and you are the ultimate inspiration behind everything I do.

To my wonderful husband: thank you for being the anchor of our home. For working those long, exhausting days so that I could have the precious gift of staying home with our little one, and for completely holding our family together while I chased this dream. Your hard work, sacrifice, and love made the space for this book to be born, and I am so deeply grateful for the life and the partnership we are building together.

To my early readers, my brilliant critique partners, and everyone who took a chance on the dark, atmospheric world of *The Midnight Cavalry*: thank you for wandering into the trenches with me. Your enthusiasm for Clara, Gideon, and the mysteries of the ridge line kept my creative fire burning.

And finally, to you, the reader. Thank you for opening this book and letting my words cast a spell on you. See you in the deep.

About the Author

Writing under the moniker Spellbounned, this author has always been drawn to the shadows where history and folklore bleed together. An avid lover of deep-woods mysteries, ancient legends, and atmospheric storytelling, she spends her time breathing life into worlds where the past is never truly dead—and the monsters are entirely too real.

When she is not writing she can be found diving into DIY projects or relaxing with a very unique, curled-eared calico cat, her pack of wild dogs or her beloved family.

A Heart in the Trenches (Book One of the Midnight Calvary Trilogy) is her debut novel.

Also by Spellbounned

Memaws Promise
Children's story about a memaws love for her grandchild.
Available on :
Amazon.com
Kindle

Nonna's Noodles
Children's story depicting a day of Nonna making handmade noodles with her grandchild.
Available on :
Amazon.com
Kindle

Nana's Bananas

Children's story showing a grand-child's day spent baking with Nana.

Available on :

Amazon.com
Kindle

Babci' Racuchy

Heartwarming children's story depicting a morning making Racuchy with Babci.

Available on :

Amazon.com
Kindle

Whimsical Weenies & Maggie the Poodle

A magical coloring book adventure inspired by the Authors two weenie dogs named Xena, Mahoon, and their poodle sister Maggie. Suitable gift for all ages! Available on Amazon.com

www.ingramcontent.com/pod-product-compliance
Lightning Source LLC
LaVergne TN
LVHW090534110826
845146LV00003B/1099
* 9 7 9 8 2 3 4 1 0 4 9 9 1 *